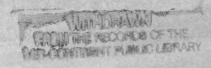

This book is dedicated to
Jigme Khyentse Rinpoche
for getting the ball rolling,
and to Rabjam Rinpoche
for giving it room to roll.

NOW I KNOW...

That we all have a jewel inside us,
somewhere.

by Sally Devorsine

Note: "Mum" is English for the American word "Mom".

First printing 2011. ISBN: 978-0-9740268-3-1

THE DALAI LAMA

ENDORSEMENT

Geshe Langri Thangpa (1054—1123 CE) was a Buddhist master famous in Tibet for his 'Eight Verses of Mind Training'. He originally wrote them down for his own personal use, but they have later become an invaluable guide for many other practitioners down the centuries. The proof of their worth is that these practical instructions on how to make oneself and others happy in everyday situations are just as relevant today, for both adults and children, as they were nearly 1,000 years ago. This I can say from my own experience, for I myself was introduced to them when I was a young boy and I have recited them every day since then. When I meet with difficult circumstances, I reflect on their meaning and I find it helpful.

Sally Devorsine teaches English in Bhutan to the young reincarnation of a lama who was one of my own esteemed teachers, Dilgo Khyentse Rinpoche. She was inspired by the verses of Langri Thangpa to create these colourful storybooks, initially to entertain her young student. Later, she realised that they might provide a way to introduce some of the longstanding values that we Tibetans hold dear to children elsewhere in the world today.

If we are to ensure a peaceful future for our world, I believe that it is important that we foster positive values like compassion, kindness and love in our children's minds from an early age. Certainly books like these can help us do that. Each of these stories shows the young reader a different way to secure happiness, whether it is by recognising anger when it arises, being aware of how our every action has an effect on others, or looking beyond our first impressions of people we meet.

I congratulate Sally Devorsine on her efforts and hope that these charming books have the edifying result she intended. I am sure they will delight readers young and old.

March 25, 2011

You could read to them...

You could help cook their dinner...

You could help them to weed the garden...

You could do the shopping for them...

You could even just make a cup of tea!

But, on Tuesday, after school, I went nextdoor.

"OK" said Mum. "You have to plan your next move very, very carefully now."

But, by lunchtime, we were quietly becoming friends.

And, on sunday, he even made me a cup of tea...

Iced... Lemon... He insisted.

When a ball suddenly landed at our feet, I even began to see things through his eyes a little.

That night I was haunted by very different memories...

Mr B[right]

twisted sad silly selfish naughty

So, when I got home, I thanked my Mum.

This book is one of a series of eight books
from the "Now I Know..." series.

Each book is based upon one of the eight verses of mind training
written by the 11th century Tibetan Buddhist master, Langri Thangpa.

Each verse, written in the back of the book, offers a different method
for finding happiness, both for ourselves and for others too.

Now I know...That I wouldn't be who I think I am, without other people.

Now I know...That I'm not, actually, Mr. Wonderful.

Now I know..That it's better to face my monsters.

Now I know...That we all have a jewel inside us somewhere.

Now I know...That I just have to look for the root and yank it out.

Now I know...That silly hopes and fears will just make wrinkles on my face.

Now I know...That it's better to keep quiet about the good things I do (and shout about the bad)

Now I know...That I just have to keep my eye on the ball.